Words to Know Before You Read

get

Mom

she

the

tip-toe

www.rourkeeducationalmedia.com

Edited by Luana K. Mitten
Illustrated by Anita DuFalla
Art Direction and Page Layout by Renee Brady

Library of Congress Cataloging-in-Publication Data

Greve, Meg
 Too Much Noise! / Meg Greve.
    p. cm. -- (Little Birdie Books)
 ISBN 978-1-61741-797-9 (hard cover) (alk. paper)
 ISBN 978-1-61236-001-0 (soft cover)
 Library of Congress Control Number: 2011924592

*Scan for Related Titles
and Teacher Resources*

Also Available as:

Rourke Educational Media
Printed in the United States of America,
North Mankato, Minnesota

rourkeeducationalmedia.com

customerservice@rourkeeducationalmedia.com • PO Box 643328 Vero Beach, Florida 32964

Too Much NOISE!

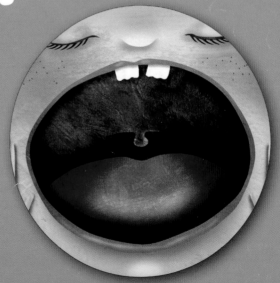

By Meg Greve

Illustrated by Anita DuFalla

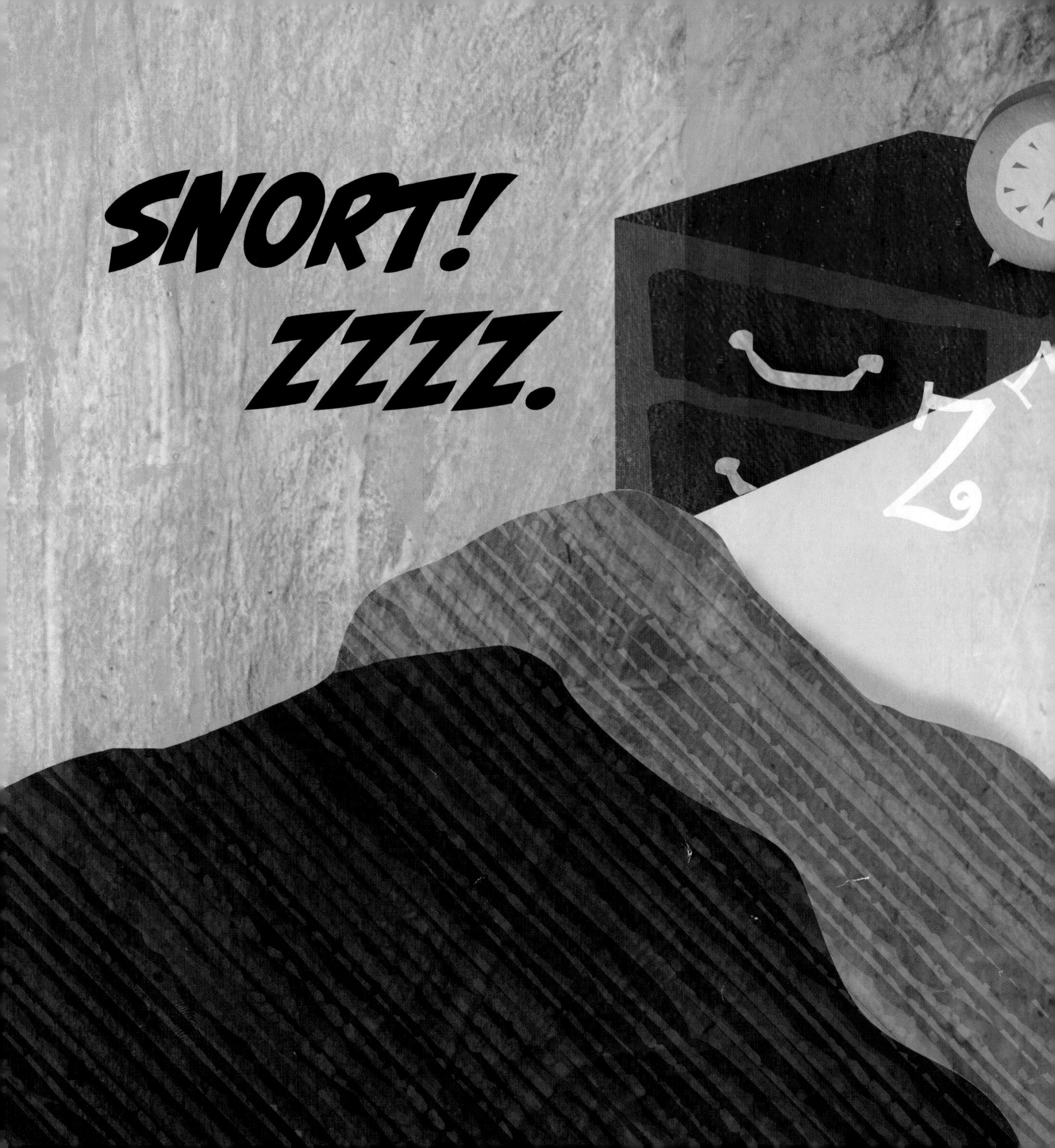
SNORT!
ZZZZ.

5

Mom is sleeping.
Shhh!

Tip-toe, tip-toe.

8

Get the bowl.

CRASH!

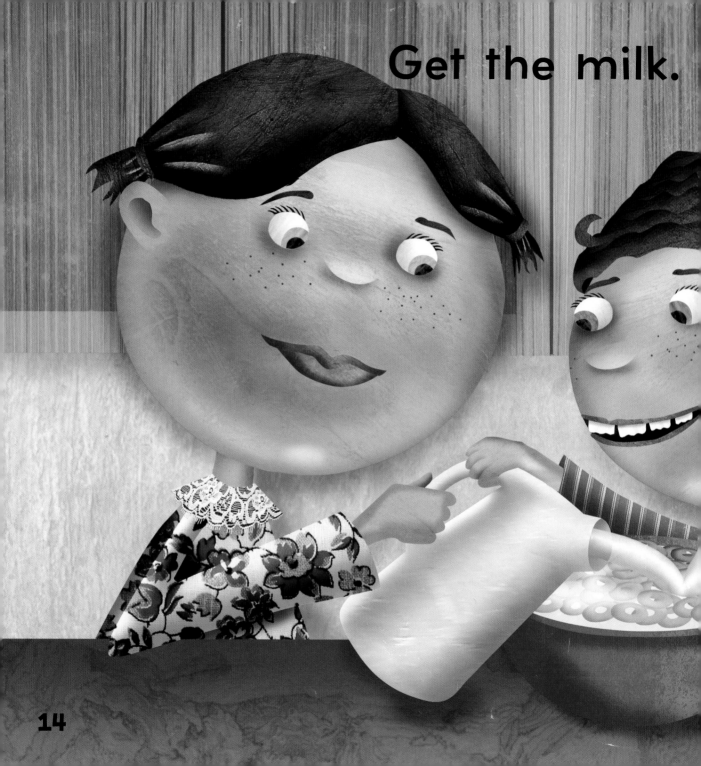

Get the milk.

14

Get the spoon.

Here she comes.

Yummy!

After Reading Activities

You and the Story...

Was the mother happy the children made breakfast for her?

Have you ever made breakfast for someone?

What can you fix for breakfast?

Words You Know Now...

On a piece of paper write each of the words below. Now write a word that rhymes with each of the words.

get

Mom

she

the

tip-toe

You Could... Make Breakfast for Someone

- Decide who you would like to make breakfast for.

- What are you going to make for breakfast?

- Make a list of all the things you will need to fix breakfast.

- Decide when and where you are going to make the breakfast.

About the Author

Meg Greve lives in Chicago with her husband, daughter, and son. On Mother's Day, her children like to serve her breakfast in bed. There is always too much noise!

Meet The Author!
www.meetREMauthors.com

About the Illustrator

Acclaimed for its versatility in style, Anita DuFalla's work has appeared in many educational books, newspaper articles, and business advertisements and on numerous posters, book and magazine covers, and even giftwraps. Anita's passion for pattern is evident in both her artwork and her collection of 400 patterned tights. She lives in the Friendship neighborhood of Pittsburgh, Pennsylvania with her son, Lucas.